# RUBY
## THE ROLY POLY LADYBUG

### ANGELA RATHKAMP

### ILLUSTRATED BY ALLISON KING

ISBN: 978-1-954095-71-7
Ruby the Roly Poly Ladybug
Copyright © 2021 by Angela Rathkamp

Illustrated by Allison King.

For permission requests, write to the publisher at the address below.

Yorkshire Publishing
1425 E 41st Pl
Tulsa, Ok 74105
www.YorkshirePublishing.com
918.394.2665

Published in the USA

# DEDICATION

This book is dedicated to my three daughters, Allison, Emily and Sarah, and my two grandchildren, Noah and Dakota. Remember you are stronger than you think you are and can do anything you set your mind to. Let God be the center of all you do. "Be strong and courageous. Do not be afraid; do not be discouraged, for the Lord your God will be with you wherever you go."
(Joshua 1:9, NIV)

Ruby, the roly-poly ladybug rolled out of her tiny bed.

She rolled right down the hallway, and then her mother said, "My sweet roly-poly Ruby, it's time to come and eat."

So, the roly-poly ladybug, rolled right up into her seat. While sitting at the table, she ate till she could eat no more. Then that roly-poly ladybug rolled back onto the floor.

4

Now it was time for school, so she gathered up her things. On her way to school that day, Ruby began to roll and sing. She sang, and she rolled, and she sang some more. She wasn't paying attention and rolled right into a store.

Mr. Beetle asked Ruby curiously, "Why do you always roll?" She glanced his way and began to say, "I just love to rock and roll." The roly-poly ladybug had to quickly be on her way. She just couldn't be late for school on such a fine spring day.

5

Now Ruby the roly-poly ladybug rolled into her school with a glow. She always had a way of putting on the grandest show. She would roll into her classroom and back out again. All of Ruby's buggy friends just sat in their chairs and grinned.

7

When it time to go back home, her teacher turned and smiled, "Ruby, my roly-poly ladybug, I will see you after a while."

The roly-poly ladybug was headed home at last. She came upon a spider who was sitting in the grass.

"Why do you always roll around?" the spider asked Ruby and grinned. The roly-poly ladybug smiled back and rolled again.

She started back on her way down the little country road. She slowed down just a little when she saw a big green toad. The toad was curious too and asked why she rolled like so. The roly-poly ladybug just shrugged and said, "I just like to, ya know?"

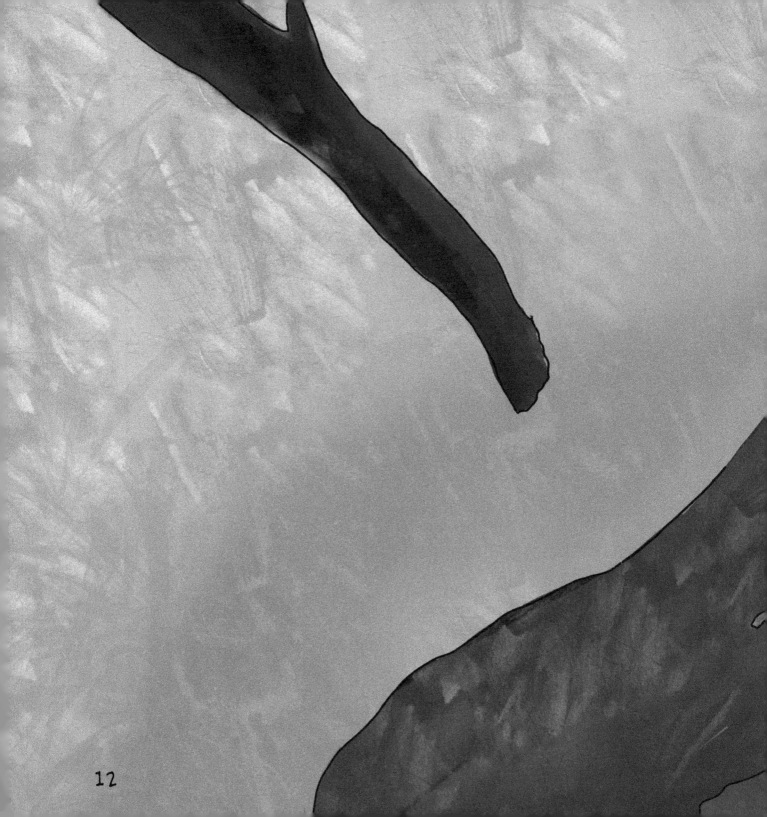

12

On down the road Ruby went as fast as she could roll. Before she even knew it she had fallen in a hole.

"What have I done?" she sadly said. "How will I ever get out?"

Ruby wasn't sure just what to do so she began to shout.

Just then an earthworm came along before she could shed a tear.

"I will help you out Ruby," the earthworm said. "Don't cry and worry, my dear."

Out of the hole, they both did go, and before the ladybug did leave, she hugged and kissed the earthworm who had saved her life indeed.

15

"I really must be on my way now. My mom is sure to worry."

The roly-poly ladybug headed down the road in a hurry. When at last she reached her own front door, she was so glad to see her mom, whom she loved and so adored.

The roly-poly ladybug gave her mom a great big hug.

Her mom just smiled and said, "Ruby you are such a wonderful little bug."

The roly-poly ladybug ate her dinner and when she was done, she rolled into the bathtub, where she splashed and had lots of fun!

Now that her day was over, the little ladybug did sigh. She rolled up onto her bed and looked out at the clear night sky. She was so very tired from her busy day that she just laid down in her bed and stared at the moon's bright ray. As she stared at the stars, Ruby began to pray.

19

"Thank you, Lord, for the wonderful world you made. Thank you for Mrs. Earthworm who saved the day. Thank you for my mommy and daddy, too. Bless all my friends and teachers. I love you."

And with that prayer, Ruby closed her eyes. Off to sleep she went with her lullabies. All snuggled up tight in her warm cozy bed, visions of a farm began to appear in her head. Feeding the goats and milking the cows, Ruby was having such fun. What an exciting day that would be for a roly-poly ladybug, playing at the farm in the sun!

The End

CPSIA information can be obtained
at www.ICGtesting.com
Printed in the USA
BVHW020900230921
617399BV00021B/581

9 781954 095717